In Pursuit of my Ancestors' Dream

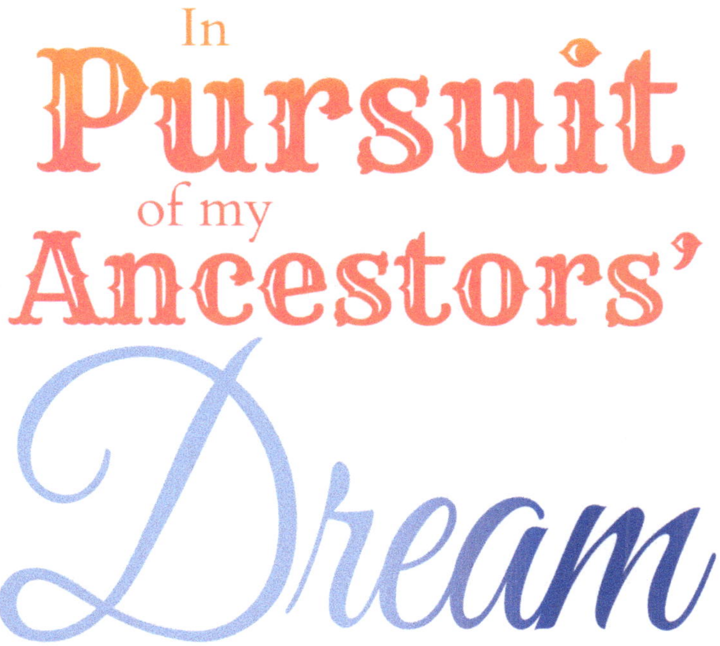

Written by: **Claude Louis, MD**
Illustrated by: **Children of Cité Soleil.**

ISBN: 978-1-962879-96-5 (Hardback)
ISBN: 978-1-962879-95-8 (Paperback)
ISBN: 978-1-962879-97-2 (E-book)

To the children of Haiti, you are our ancestors' dream. With education and a bit of humanity, we can reach that potential. I stand with you!

Thank you to my history teachers for planting a seed.

Merci AFORC and our four illustrators.

Merci Marc Elie Saint Vil, Jean Adler Rousseau and Cité Soleil high school principal (Olgé).

Today, Principal Fignolé told us we could be anything.

He said every child is precious and gifted in their own way—even those like us from the slums.

I raised my hand and asked, "What about the children with no home or parents? What can they achieve without love, education, and support?"

Principal Fignolé smiled wide and nodded: "Françoise Péralte, it's true the apple never falls far from the tree. It must run in your blood."

Then he announced that the debate team was recruiting.

"Qui veut Juin prépare Septembre"
Nb 23
Pr 21
Ab 2
Nou se Prens ak Prensès

I am Françoise Péralte from Cité Soleil. I am only twelve, but there are so many things I dream of being.

As a singer or songwriter, I'd write and sing about homeless children from slums like mine. I'd tell the world of their strength and courage.

As a lawyer, I'd advocate that they, too, have rights.

As a doctor, I'd dress their wounds and ease their suffering.

And as a teacher, I'd show them how to read, write, and achieve their dreams.

Do they know what they've been missing? In a world with so many inspiring stories, which characters could've been their role models?

Do they know they are descendants of queens and kings? That even in poverty, they are the children of the first freedom fighters?

Maybe one day I can become Madame President, the Dream Maker.

I ran home, my heart pumping with excitement.

"Mom, I can get elected as Kid President. But first I need to become team captain."

"You're right, Frankie. You can become anything! But what's a team captain?"

"It's the leader of our school's debate team! If we win the national final, I can be elected Kid President."

"But what does the Kid President do, Frankie?"

"Every year, a Kid President is elected to be the voice of the youth in the country. Most kids want to be the Kid President because they get to do cool stuff like tour amusement parks, meet celebrities, and go on TV. Last year, the boy who won even got to hang out with Cristiano Ronaldo."

"Wow! I can see why you want the job."

"Mom, it's not about the perks! I want to become Kid President so I can tell adult leaders what kids need in the slums. I want to make the country a better place for everyone, especially the kids whose voices aren't heard."

My mother took me in her arms and shook her head in astonishment. "You remind me so much of your father. He was a selfless man with an amazing heart."

The next day at school, Jean, the captain from the previous year, laughed at my dream. "You want to be Kid President? Are you nuts? Surely you know you have no shot. First, you're from the slums. Second, you're a girl. There's never been a girl Kid President. Not one! Plus, you'd have to beat me to take my place as captain. And that will never happen."

I covered my face so Jean would not notice my tears. I could not stand him, but deep inside I knew he had a point.

"What about all the brave women in history who accomplished what they were told was impossible?" I asked myself.

That night, I went to bed with a heavy heart.

As I fell into a slumber, I floated through a white veil and found myself surrounded by strange people in funny clothing. It took me a moment to realize who they were: warriors who had fought for my country's freedom.

Suddenly, a feminine voice softly whispered in my ears.

"You can do this," the voice said. "You were born for this. A thousand footsteps have led to where you stand now."

The following day, Jean and I debated in front of the entire school for the team captainship. Jean believed that Dessalines had been far more instrumental than Toussaint in the fight for Haiti's independence. I retorted that one was the egg and the other was the chicken. Neither could exist without the other, nor could Haiti.

When I finished my rebuttal, the audience erupted in applause. I had won the fight and became the first girl team captain of my school!

Jean threatened to quit the team, but I convinced him we'd be better off if we stuck together, just like Toussaint and Dessalines did in spite of their differences. So he stayed.

As captain, I knew I had to be extra prepared, so I stayed up late after finishing my chores to study. Sitting under an old kerosene lamp—my house had no electricity—I read additional books about history, my ancestors, and my culture. Slowly, my knowledge broadened, and I encouraged my teammates to do the same.

While our future opponents would have access to the wealth of knowledge on the internet, all we had was our local community library, which was filled with old, overused books. But this didn't mean we couldn't win.

"Knowledge is universal," I told my teammates. "They are not smarter than us. The only thing that matters is the accuracy of the information, not how we obtain it. With practice, hard work, and focus, we can beat any team. We will not fear them. We are the princesses and princes of Cité Soleil!"

Soon, we marched on to challenge the best schools in the country.

And we won, over and over again.

Against Saint-Louis de Gonzague, we, the princesses and princes of Cité Soleil, swung our rebuttals like a racket, hitting our opponents with vicious backhands like Naomi Osaka. We scored an easy victory.

At Notre Dame in Cap-Haitian, we dribbled our arguments in a mix of Creole and French past the competition, dodging rebuttals with the skills of Melchie Dumornay, and sent our closing argument sailing like a beautiful chip shot over the goalie. Another victory!

When we faced Mères de Bourdon in the third round, our speeches flowed like the prose of Edwidge Danticat, whose protagonists echo the melancholic but resilient nature of the Haitian people. Like them, we never gave up. We are unbreakable, just like our ancestors.

While facing Canado High School in the quarterfinals, our rhythm flowed like the beautiful song "Dyaman Nan Bidonvil" by ZAFEM. With Dener Ceide's mystical guitar filling the soundscape, the song compares children in the streets and slums with diamonds. We spoke with the same passion, our words sending the audience to tears.

Our team of five underdogs went on to demolish the debate team of Lycée Alexandre Pétion. Our voices echoed like Rara music's vuvuzelas and vaksines, the great Haitian trumpets made of bamboo.

And like a high-decibel carnival float on Champ-de-Mars, we marched all the way to the debate finale.

There we'd face Le Lycée Français d'Haïti, the school that had won the most national trophies. They had once even claimed victory over Le Lycée de Paris. Achieving victory would be difficult.

But suddenly, right before the finale, we suffered a major blow: Jude, one of our best debaters, announced he could no longer participate. His father had been kidnapped by the gangs, and his family could not afford the ransom.

Principal Fignolé called us into his office.

"It does not matter now which team wins the finale. As far as Cité Soleil and the country are concerned, you've already won. As a community, we will come together to support Jude's family. Your only job is to debate your hearts out."

The night before the finale, I was too agitated and scared to sleep. When I finally drifted off, I saw the face of Dessalines in my dreams. He spoke to me with a quiet, fierce determination.

"We earned our independence with our blood. Many of my fellow generals died, but we fought until victory was won! We did it for you and all the children of Cité Soleil and Haiti. Go my daughter, go! Tell them that the ransom for our independence, our freedom from the colonial forces of France, has stunted the growth of my beautiful children. For this country to regain its prosperity, France must pay our people and our nation back in full!"

Général Dessalines

Bibliyotèk

The Student Debate Finale was a huge event. People traveled hundreds of miles to witness the debate and meet the country's future leaders. Every social media site broadcasted the event live. National news outlets tuned in. Anticipation built.

One by one, teams were eliminated from the competition. Finally, only two remained.

Our team and the team from Le Lycée Français sat down and stared out at the sea of faces. All eyes were on us: a team of four against a team of five. We, the underdogs, were also outnumbered.

Behind their gleaming laptops, expensive glasses, and designer clothing, Le Lycée Français was eager to celebrate an early victory. Surely, they thought, Jude's absence would give them the edge heading into the closing arguments. But then Jean stood up and gave a passionate speech about social injustice and the disparities between our team and our opponents. The teams appeared more even than anyone had previously thought.

Finally, it was time for the closing arguments. One of the judges asked, "How do we make our ancestors' dream come true?" He called me up first to speak.

After a deep sigh and an anxious moment of silence, I stood up and walked to the microphone.

"If education is freedom, then Haiti is not quite free yet. How can every child receive an education if we do not have the resources? And if freedom is a state of mind, then the path to freedom must be education. Take a look out of this building to see our children, our streets and living conditions! Our ancestors had a dream. They wanted us not just free physically but free to become the masters of our destiny!

Our teammate Jude is not with us today, for his father has been kidnapped by the gangs. Before, he drove a tap tap and struggled to make a living. Now his poor family will have to sell everything they own and borrow money with interest to rescue him. Otherwise, they will never afford to pay those criminals.

Gang violence is a modern curse. But have our people ever been free of gangs? When French soldiers came in 1825 and threatened to reestablish slavery unless we paid a ransom, they were just gangs in uniforms. Jude's family will spend their lives working to pay a debt they never owed. And the same is true for Haiti.

People often ask, 'Why is Haiti so poor?' Well, I ask in return, 'Why does a well run dry?' If you take and take, eventually you will hit the bottom. For too long, people have taken from Haiti and pushed our people to take from one another. They have pushed us, believing all our hope would drain away. The money we could have used to build a prosperous nation instead enriched those who had already stolen the humanity of our ancestors. They destroyed our future and ruined our freedom. But within each of us is a well that runs so deep that nothing can empty it. A well of hope. A well of dreams. And with knowledge and education, freedom will be ours once more!"

A silence enveloped the entire auditorium. There was no applause this time—only tremors and tears. The judges watched on with wide eyes. During debates, students rarely spoke of such things.

The captain of the opposing team stood up and started clapping. Le Lycée Français conceded defeat. "You make our ancestors proud!" he added. The whole audience stood up, joining in the applause.

The jury stood too and crowned me, Françoise, the Cité Soleil princess, as the nation's new and first female Kid President. The dream I'd wanted had come true.

When I returned home, I gave my trophy to my mother.

"That's yours, Mom!" I said.

I thought about my father, who had always said I would one day do great things. He had lost his life fighting to achieve his own dream: to travel overseas and earn money for his family. But the boat he'd traveled upon did not hold up, and so, he was not there to witness.

I picked up the juiciest mango I could find from the trees in the slums. I knew I needed to celebrate with the sweetest of fruits. I bit into it and sucked up the juice until only the seed remained in my palms. Then I planted it in the rich, dark soil beneath me.

With a little hope and love, it might one day become a great tree.

After the finale, my speech was shared throughout the nation. Soon it gained attention throughout
the rest of the world.

People signed petitions and marched in the streets
across the globe. They urged France to return the
ransom, to pay Haiti what it deserved.

Politicians and leaders called for justice for
historical crimes France had committed.

With a whole nation behind me, the little girl from Cité Soleil, traveled to the ancient city across the sea: Paris. There I sat with the French president. As the Kid President representing every child of my nation, I presented my request to him.

"It's a moral obligation, Mr. President. You and your country must undo this unjust act so that you can truly become what you claim to be: Le Bastion de la Liberté. Until then, you will never be the true Bastion of Freedom."

"The luxurious life you have created here has in part been built on the backs of my ancestors," I said before the French Parliament. "I come to claim the ransom we were forced to pay for our independence. With that money, we will rebuild our country and make sure every child in the streets has a home, an education, leisure, and everything else a child in France enjoys. That is also how we will resolve the gang problem. We will build universities, hospitals, and roads. We will invest in our own development to take care of our people, just as you do here."

The representatives listened on, and I could see they felt sad and angry, but mainly ashamed. The majority voted in favor of working on a document to pay restitution owed to Haiti.

Almost overnight, I became a global figure. While in France, a major TV channel interviewed me, then organized a telethon that collected tens of thousands of dollars that would go directly to programs helping children in Haiti's streets and the most vulnerable slums. All the while, the world waited for the French government to make its final decision regarding the moral and financial debt to Haiti.

My next stop was the United States. CNN interviewed me about my unlikely heroic journey to France. But I wasn't done, I told them. I planned to go to the US Congress next to inquire about Haiti's gold reserve, which was taken away by US marines in 1914, and the assassination of my great-grandfather, Charlemagne Péralte during the occupation for standing up for his country.

les enfants
d'Haïti
l'invité

In less than a year, the world saw that anything was possible for the Haitian people. If I could dream, so could they.

Back in Haiti, I took the debate team with me to the attractive coastal beaches of Port-Salut—a prize I'd won for becoming Kid President. Jude even joined us, our prize money having paid his father's ransom. The water and sky were as blue as our smiles were wide. One day, perhaps, the beautiful south will become one of the greatest tourist destinations in the world. For this, education thus freedom, I dream.

This story was inspired by questions I had as an inquisitive twelve-year-old. My interest in history prompted many conversations with my teachers after class, and they fed my curiosity. I studied long hours at night under the dim light of a candle, and I took pride in repeating passages from memory the following day in front of the class. Every battle, every victory—I couldn't wait to learn what happened next. How incredible that a former slave became a leader and raised an army that defeated the strongest army in the world! I innocently looked up to those heroes. After all, they looked just like me.

France controlled Saint-Domingue (now Haiti) for over a century until the Haitian Revolution began toward the end of the eighteenth century. When the French cowardly took General Toussaint Louverture hostage in 1802, Toussaint warned the French soldiers that he was but a tree trunk whose roots would grow back. Less than two years later, the Haitian indigenous army defeated Napoleon Bonaparte's army to become the first Black republic and the only successful group of slaves to have fought and defeated their oppressors to claim their freedom.

Two decades later in 1825, France threatened to invade and reinstate slavery if the Haitian government refused to pay an indemnity of $28 billion, or up to $115 billion in today's money according to the *New York Times*. Haiti struggled for 122 years to pay the ransom, with interest financed through French banks accounting for approximately 80% of its GDP annually, leaving very little for infrastructure, health care, or education. Poor farmers had to collect little they had to contribute to pay France. In addition, the US invaded Haiti from 1915 to 1934, took its gold reserve, and had complete control of Haiti's finances.

In Pursuit of My Ancestors' Dream is the cry of the children of Haiti. Through Françoise, a little girl from Cité Soleil, the world will hear our cry for justice, for restitution and reparations, equality and human dignity. Every child in Cité Soleil is entitled to the same opportunities as those of Paris, Washington DC or anywhere in the world. That's what our ancestors envisioned.

Françoise, this book's four illustrators, and I are just a few of the roots Toussaint Louverture referred to. In his name and that of all of our ancestors with the same voice, we are all calling on France to pay Haiti back, in full, the double debt that was forced upon Haiti after gaining its freedom.

After two hundred years of misfortune and crippled development caused in part by this immoral act, we Haitians deserve to start again. This is the call for a revolution. Our second revolution. Not one with arms or for revenge, but this time, with hope for a final turn toward prosperity for Haiti's children.

About the author:

Claude Louis is a physician. He is the founder of Words In Action Haiti. He writes children's books in English, French and his native Haitian Creole to share his culture and stories with the rest of the world. All proceeds from his book sales go directly to support children education initiatives in Kenscoff and at-risk areas in Port au Prince.

He is also the author of I'm All Grown Now Papa, When Kais Met Toussaint, Je ne Suis plus un Gamin Papa/Mwen Finn Grandi Net Papa, The Voodoo Princess and the Despicable Troll, La Princesse Vaudou et le Vilain Troll.

To learn more, visit www.wiahaiti.org/ Words in Action Facebook/Claude Louis(author facebook page).

More books:

Je Ne Suis Plus Un Gamin Papa
Mwen Finn Grandi Nèt Papa
Histoire vraie de l'enfance de Claude Louis
Istwa Lavi Tiklod
Écrit par Claude Louis   Illustré par Junior Michel

I'm All Grown Now, Papa
WRITTEN BY Claude Louis, MD   ILLUSTRATED BY Junior Michel

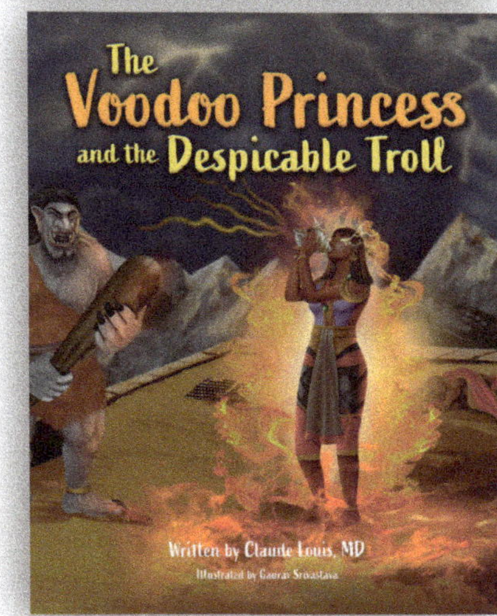

The Voodoo Princess and the Despicable Troll
Written by Claude Louis, MD
Illustrated by Gaurav Srivastava

La Princesse Vaudou et le Vilain Troll
Écrit par Claude Louis, MD
Illustré par Gaurav Srivastava

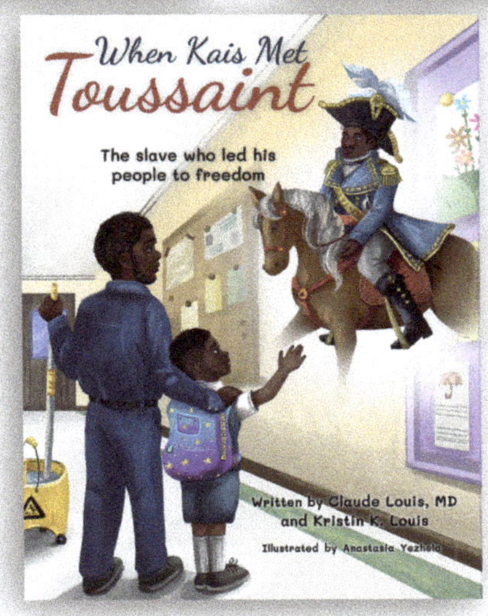

When Kais Met Toussaint
The slave who led his people to freedom
Written by Claude Louis, MD
and Kristin K. Louis
Illustrated by Anastasia Yezhova

Illustrators

This book is illustrated by four gifted teenage boys from Cité Soleil guided by a local artist.

Who else would be more qualified to paint the reality in Haiti than its own children? Through the public school of Cité Soleil and the local youth organization AFORC (Atelier de Formation et de Créativité), a drawing contest that started with thirty children, led to four finalists. Then, a workshop was held throughout the summer of 2022 into the next calendar year as school reopening was delayed because of gang violence. For three days a week, up to three hundred children found refuge in a school where they played, performed comedy sketches, drew, danced, ate two meals and forgot their problems temporarily. Our goal is to use the profit from this work to tap into education and art projects for skill development for the local children through AFORC.

Roblin Pierre Risson; François Habaccuc; Charles Alix; Joseph Edson.

Glossary

Vuvuzela: Long horn type instrument when blown into, produces a loud sound.

Vaksine: Scarved bamboo used as musical instrument.

Champ-de-Mars: Large park in front of Haiti's national palace.

Rara: Haitian music where bands parade for miles with multiple stops as bystanders gather and follow while singing and dancing along.

Konpa: Dance music originated in Haiti

Tap tap: colorful pick-up trucks or buses used as means of transportation in Haiti.

ZAFEM: Popular Konpa band founded by two friends: lead singer Réginald Cangé and Dener Ceide.